SALLY GRINDLEY

Mulberry

goes to school

Illustrated by Tania Hurt-Newton

MACDONALD YOUNG BOOKS

LEABHARLANN CHONTAE MHUIGHEO

This book may be kept for two weeks. It may
be renewed if not required by another borrower.
The latest date entered is the date by which the
book should be returned.

Text copyright © Sally Grindley 2000
Illustrations copyright © Tania Hurt-Newton 2000

First published in Great Britain in 2000
by Macdonald Young Books
an imprint of Wayland Publishers Ltd
an imprint of Hodder Headline
338 Euston Road
London NW1 3BH

The right of Sally Grindley to be identified as the author
of this Work and the right of Tania Hurt-Newton to be
identified as the illustrator of this Work has been asserted
by them in accordance with the Copyright, Designs and
Patents Act 1988.

Designed and typeset by Danny McBride
Printed in Hong Kong by Wing King Tong

British Library Cataloguing in Publication Data available

ISBN: 0 7500 2914 5

Mulberry sat in the car and wagged his tail.
"Can I come, too?" he barked as they jumped out of the car.

"Stay, Mulberry," they said. But they forgot to close the door.

Mulberry jumped out and ran through the gate after them.

Some children were playing with a ball. Mulberry trotted over to them.

The children laughed and threw
the ball backwards and forwards
over his head.

Can I play?

Mulberry jumped and missed – GRRR!
jumped and missed – GRRRR!
jumped and – caught it.

"Good doggy, give it back," they said.
"I want to keep it," barked Mulberry.
Then he heard someone shout his name
and he ran away again.

Some children were skipping. Mulberry watched them swing the rope round. Then he grabbed it in his mouth and ran off.

Then a bell rang. CLANG, CLANG, CLANG!
Mulberry was frightened. He saw an open door and ran through it – BUMP! – right into a man with a broom.

"I've just cleaned that floor!" shouted the man.

Mulberry didn't like cross voices.
He dashed into an empty room
and hid.

Nobody came after him. Mulberry peeped out. At the back of the classroom was a table with a cage on it.

"There's a hamster in there," he barked.

The hamster poked its nose out of its
nest. Mulberry ran round and round
the cage.
"Let's play!" he barked.

But the hamster went back to sleep.
"You're no fun," whined Mulberry.

Mulberry heard footsteps. He dashed out of the room. He ran through another door, and another. He found himself in a hall full of children.

Some of them were climbing up
the wall.
Some of them were rolling on mats.
Some of them were touching their toes.

Mulberry rolled on the mats. He jumped over the benches. He ran round and round in circles. The children giggled, then a loud voice said, "What's that dog doing in here?"

Mulberry didn't like cross voices.
He ran out of the hall and into
a cloakroom.

Mulberry found a shoe and gave it a good chew. He found a tin that rattled when he shook it. Then he sniffed and found a box full of food. He shook off the lid and bit into a cheese sandwich.

A boy came into the cloakroom. When he saw Mulberry he started to cry.

"Have I been naughty?" whined Mulberry, and ran away.

Mulberry found an open door and went inside. It was dark. He bumped into a big monster machine and growled at it.

Mulberry didn't like the look of it. He stepped back and got his paw tangled in the wire. When he pulled at it, something fell on his head.

Then the door slammed shut – BANG!
– and Mulberry couldn't see a thing.
He howled and howled, but nobody
came. His head was sore and his paw
was sore.

"I want to go home," he howled.
"I want my doggy basket and my
chewy bone and my squeaky ball."

But nobody came. Mulberry curled up
and soon he was fast asleep.

Mulberry woke up when the door opened and a light went on. He jumped to his feet, barked loudly, and licked the teacher standing at the door.

Then he rushed out of the room and ran down the corridor.

Mulberry ran straight into a bucket of
water – BUMP! – and knocked it over.

Then he ran into a girl and knocked
her over.

At last he came to a door.
It was closed.
"Let me out," he howled.

Mulberry scratched the door.
"I want to go home," he howled.

27

Suddenly the door opened and there they were. Mulberry jumped up and wagged his tail.

"Naughty dog," they said. "Dogs don't go to school."
Mulberry hung his head and dropped his tail. He wanted kind words.

"Home, Mulberry," they said.
"Yes, please," barked Mulberry.

Mulberry ran to the car. As soon as
the door was open, he jumped inside.
He sat on the seat and wagged his tail.
"Let's go home," he barked. "It's time
for my doggy crunchy things."

Look out for more of Mulberry's adventures:

Mulberry Goes to Town by Sally Grindley
Mulberry's out on the town. He's having a great time
eating buns and growling at the teddies in the toy shop.
But why does everyone keep chasing him away? When he
has a nasty brush with some moving stairs, Mulberry
decides that he's had enough of shopping.

Mulberry Alone at the Seaside by Sally Grindley
Mulberry has come to the seaside. He has great fun
splashing in the sea and knocking down sand-castles. He
even helps himself to someone's picnic. But when Mulberry
is trapped by the tide, he decides he's had enough of the
seaside for one day.

Mulberry Alone on the Farm by Sally Grindley
Mulberry visits a farm for the day. He runs off to look for
someone to play with, but the hens, the piglets and the
scarecrow don't want to play with him. Mulberry is fed up,
until the sky grows dark and he gets caught in a scary
thunderstorm.

All these books in the Mulberry series can be purchased
from your local bookseller. For more information about
Mulberry, write to: *The Sales Department, Hodder Headline,
338 Euston Road, London NW1 3BH.*